Erie Cousins

Dorothy Stacy

Erie Canal Cousins

by
Dorothy Stacy

Blackberry Hill Press
Sauquoit, New York

Library of Congress Control Number: 2007900315

ISBN-13: 978-0-9792947-0-9

Illustrations by the author

Published by
Blackberry Hill Press
2860 Mohawk Street
Sauquoit, New York

Printed in the U.S.A. by
Morris Publishing
3212 East Highway 30
Kearney, NE 68847
1-800-650-7888

This book is dedicated to....
my husband, John L. Stacy III
my children,
Jerilyn, Kim, Karen, Gabi, Kathy, Matt, Jack, Pat
and my parents, Vincent and Helen Dmochowski

Special thanks to...

Karen Tucker, my daughter, for editing the manuscript, helping me with the computer work, and giving me some advice concerning the artwork.

My husband, who listened to me read and talk about the manuscript, urged me to go on when discouraged, and is my strongest supporter.

My daughters, Jerilyn and Kathy, for reading and commenting on the on the manuscript.

Janet Davis and Donna Jarmak, fellow teachers at St. Peter's School, for taking the time to read my manuscript and comment on it and Janet Davis for doing some editing of the manuscript.

The helpful staff at the Oneida County Historical Society and the Utica Public Library where I did some of the research for my book.

My students at St. Peter's School for listening to the story before it became a book.

The great staff at Morris Publishing for being helpful and supportive each time I called.

Author's Note

The day I took my first-grade class on a field trip to the Erie Canal Village in Rome, New York, I began to wonder what life would have been like there in the 1800s. I became aware of how calm and peaceful I felt on the packet boat ride, and how much I enjoyed strolling through the re-created 1850's village. Learning about the building of the canal, I realized what a marvelous feat its construction had been in that day and age. I began to research the era and the canal extensively, and that inspired me to write this book.

Erie Canal Cousins presents history to children in an interesting, entertaining way. It is full of adventures typical of early travel on the Erie Canal including boat life, low bridges, locks, hoggees, ghost stories, and much more.

The story of Rose is a work of fiction set in a historical period. It is typical of a girl who would have lived at that time in that place. The characters are fictitious and resemblance to anyone living or dead is purely coincidental. However, the Erie Canal *is* real, and the facts about it are true. I have tried to be as historically accurate as possible in telling this story.

Contents

Rose Stewart

Chapter 1
The Glorious Trip

Wednesday, August 5, 1840
Albany, New York

I, Rose Stewart, will be traveling on the Grand Canal tomorrow with Mama. We will be going to Utica to help my Aunt Jenny with her three little boys and the new baby. I have never been on a boat in all of my thirteen years of life. Nor have I ever been to Utica. So I reckon it will be quite an adventure.

It is long past my bedtime as I write this, but I have been unable to sleep. It's as though a current is swirling throughout my body, and I can't lay still. I want it to be tomorrow. The time passes too slowly. I know I'll be tired in the morning, but I'm helpless to do otherwise.

My greatest wish is to see the canal that everyone has been raving about. I've been wishing for this on every hay load or first star I see. Now it's finally going to come true.

I will also be meeting my cousins Bridget, Tom, and Sean. They live on the boat with Uncle Dermot and Aunt

Cora. My uncle offered us passage from Albany on his boat, the Flying Eagle, as he often delivers goods to Syracuse and has to go right past Utica. We will meet him at the dock at four o'clock in the afternoon.

The Erie Canal was finished two years before I was born. Yorkers all complained and called it Clinton's Ditch or Clinton's Folly before it was done, but now people can't say enough good things about it. I reckon it wasn't such a bad idea Governor DeWitt Clinton had after all.

I am going to be a writer like Papa some day, so I want to record everything about this trip in my new journal.

Rose

With that, Rose closed the book, put the pen away, and blew out the candle. She got into bed and tried to settle down again. Cassie, her sister, was still asleep in the other bed. That girl could sleep through a storm. As soon as Rose closed her eyes, she began to see boats, water, trunks, and the likes. She could almost *smell* the water. Sakes alive, it would be a rip-roaring trip!

Just as she was finally about to drift off to sleep, Rose heard a loud crash and then screams coming from the boy's bedroom. She jumped up and ran, nearly colliding with Mama and Papa as they all charged into the room together.

"It hurts! It hurts!" Caleb lay on the floor holding his leg, which was already swollen to twice its normal size.

"John, quick go get Doc Davis." Mama's voice was almost as loud as Caleb's was. "I know I shouldn't have let him sleep on the top bunk of the bed, but he begged so. He's just too small."

Papa had his coat on and was out the door before she finished her last sentence. The doctor lived just two houses down from them, but it took him a while to wake, get dressed, and return with his black bag.

Meanwhile Mama and Rose tried to console Caleb by singing to him until they returned. Robert, still asleep in the bottom bunk, seemed oblivious to the whole situation.

After examining Caleb, the doctor shook his head and said, "I believe he has a nasty break there, Mrs. Stewart. I can set and splint it, but you'll have to watch him carefully till that swelling starts going down some. Even then, you'll have to keep that rambunctious four-year-old off of that foot for a good six weeks or more."

"I can do that," said Mama.

Papa walked Doc Davis to the door and apologized for getting him out of bed at the ungodly hour of one A.M., as he let him out.

"But, Mama, we're supposed to go on our trip tomorrow," blurted Rose, not realizing how selfish that sounded until it was out of her mouth.

"Don't go, Mama," Caleb wailed. "I want you here with me."

"Don't worry, darlin', I won't leave you."

"But what about Aunt Jenny?" Rose protested weakly.

"Mama can't go on the trip, but you can go in her place. You're a strong girl, a hard worker, and have a way with the little ones. You will be a big help to Aunt Jenny," said Papa, congratulating himself for solving the problem so quickly.

"No, no, Papa. I can't go alone."

"You won't be alone. You'll be with your aunt and uncle and cousins."

"But I don't know any of them, and I've never been on a boat, and I...I can't even swim."

"You'll be fine, Rosie, you worry too much. I'll bring you to the dock and hand you right over to Uncle Dermot." Papa tried to reason with her.

"Can I bring Cassie with me in Mama's place?" Rose hoped against hope that her eleven-year-old sister could go with her.

"I'm sorry, honey, I'll need Cassie here to help me with the chores now that I'll have to tend to Caleb," Mama said.

"I think we all need to get some sleep now. We'll talk more about this in the morning." Papa left to go to his own room while Mama decided to stay with Caleb. Rose made her way back to the girl's bedroom.

"I *won't* go," Rose said softly, under her breath. Her stomach felt as if someone were trying to scramble eggs in it when she lay down this time. Now her thoughts were fearful. *Who would she talk to? What if she fell off the*

4

boat? What if she acted silly and they laughed at her? Could she dare say no to Papa? She finally fell asleep, but slept fitfully the rest of the night.

When she awoke, Rose tiptoed softly into the boy's room and saw that Mama was curled up on the floor right next to Caleb. They were still asleep. She paused before the hall mirror to splash some water on her face and comb her long, coal-black tresses. She looked so much like Papa with her fair skin and blue eyes. Cassie and Robert took after Mama by way of their curly red hair, freckles, and green eyes. Caleb had a little bit of both Mama and Papa's features in him. She ventured into Papa's room thinking she might convince him to call off the trip.

"Good morning, Rosie."

"Good morning, Papa."

"Now what's this nonsense about you not wanting to go on this canal trip? I thought you were hankering to do this for a long time now."

"That was before Caleb got hurt."

"What does that have to do with it?"

"Well, now Mama can't go and I'm uneasy about traveling on my own."

"You'll be fine."

"You'll be with your aunt, uncle, and cousins," they both said together, and Papa laughed, but Rose felt even more anxious at that thought.

5

"Rosie, you'll be fascinated with the Erie Canal once you see it. Let me tell you a little story about its opening:

"In October of 1825, when the canal was finished, there was a big celebration planned. Your mother and I had just been married, and we went down to the dock in Albany to see it. There was a 24-gun salute, speeches at the Capitol Building, and outdoor dinners on the Columbia St. Bridge. What a grand time it was.

Governor De Witt Clinton boarded a packet boat called the Seneca Chief and led a fleet of four boats down the Erie Canal, starting at Buffalo all the way to Albany and then down the Hudson River to New York City. All up and down the canal there was partying. Villages and towns had been making preparations for it since summer. Crowds lined up all along the banks and cheered, gun salutes pierced the air, and many places shot off fireworks. At the beginning of the event, a cannon in Buffalo was fired. Other cannons placed along the way, in turn, were fired when they each heard the preceding one go off. It took about one hour and twenty minutes for the signal to get to New York and back."

"That sounds thrilling! What else happened?" Rose was beginning to lighten up a bit.

"More and more boats joined the fleet as they traveled along. After a big celebration in Albany, two powerful steamboats towed all of them down the Hudson River to New York City. Ships from many nations joined in the festivities there. That is where the wedding ceremony took place."

"Wedding ceremony?" Rose was puzzled. "Who got married?"

Papa laughed, "Not that kind of wedding. It was the *Wedding of the Waters*. Governor Clinton poured water that he brought in kegs from Lake Erie, into the Atlantic Ocean to show that the two were now united."

"That is fascinating, Papa. Do tell more." Rose's curiosity was beginning to outdo her qualms about the trip.

"Well, in New York, besides the wedding ceremony, there was a Grand Canal Ball, fireworks, and a parade. Do you know that President John Q. Adams was there, as well as, former presidents John Adams, Thomas Jefferson, James Madison, and James Monroe?"

By this time Mama had entered the room and was listening to Papa tell the end of the story.

"Oh, Mama, that is such an exciting story," said Rose. It's made me feel a bit better about the trip, but I'm still not sure I want to go."

"You'll like Utica," said Mama. "Aunt Jenny writes that it is one of the most flourishing cities in New York and is quite developed. It has several newspapers, dry-goods stores, groceries, inns, and a population of almost 13,000 people."

"I have an idea," continued Mama. "Why don't you write about the trip in your new journal, so you can remember it and share it with us when you get back? And if you're frightened or lonely, you can write about that too, so you can let it out, and it'll make you feel better. Just pretend you're talking to me when you write." Mama tried to be helpful, knowing how timid her eldest daughter was.

"What a great idea," said Rose. Now she felt like she might be able to bear it. Perhaps it would not be easy with her shyness, but at least she was more optimistic about the trip now.

Chapter 2
Meeting the Cousins

For better or worse, I am going on the trip. Mama and Papa have made the decision. They can't say enough good things about the Erie Canal and Utica. I hope I like my cousins especially the girl, Bridget, who is my age.

I am thankful to Mama for giving me this beautiful journal for my birthday last month in my favorite color, too. Mama told me she took a plain journal, padded it with cotton, and covered the whole thing with pretty blue calico cloth. Then she put some white cloth, bordered in lace, on the front cover and stitched my initials in the middle. She also sewed a pocket in the back cover to hold my quills and any other treasures I might want to put in there.

I must go now. Papa is calling and we are ready to leave for the docks. The newspaper gave him the day off, so he could escort me there.

Rose

Rose and Papa stood in the harbor looking for the *Flying Eagle*. The canal was filled with all kinds of boats as far as the eye could see. The sun was shining and the sky was bright blue with very few clouds.

"I didn't know there were that many different boats," said Rose.

"There sure are. There's the packet, which usually carries passengers for long distances. There's one over there." Papa pointed to a long, slender, streamlined craft. "It's always very colorful to attract customers."

"I *do* like the bright yellow and blue paint," Rose stated.

"Then there are line boats. Many of the families who live on these boats own them. They carry merchandise as well as a few passengers. Often they are used to carry families who want to move westward."

"Are there any other kinds?"

"I'm sure there are, but those are the only two I'm familiar with. You'll have to ask Uncle Dermot about the others when you get on the boat."

"Look!" cried Rose. "There's the *Flying Eagle*."

The sleek red and white boat towed by two mules drifted slowly into the harbor. Flower boxes full of red geraniums and fluffy white curtains decorated the cabin windows. A large sign up top bearing the name, *Flying Eagle*, proclaimed, indeed, that it was the boat they were looking for.

"We're over here," Papa and Rose shouted in unison and waved. They ran down the shore until they were closer to the boat, so Uncle Dermot would see them. Soon they were along side of the vessel.

"John, John," a large booming voice called out. "Come aboard."

Papa and Rose jumped over the short span of water and were soon standing next to a tall, heavy-set man with curly red hair, beard, and mustache, who, underneath it all, resembled her mother. Next to him was a slight woman with sandy hair who only came up to his shoulder. A petite girl with a devilish grin and the same hair as her father stood barefoot along side her mother. A red-headed, little boy made up the rest of the foursome.

"Welcome aboard, John, but where's Darcy?" Uncle Dermot looked past them, thinking she might be lagging behind.

"Unfortunately Darcy won't be able to make the trip. Caleb fell out of bed last night and broke his leg, so Rose here will have to go in her place."

"Oh, no. I was so looking forward to seeing my sister again." Uncle Dermot's face fell for a second at the news, but then he focused his attention on Rose. "So this is your Rose. A beauty she is," the big man boomed once more.

"Yes, this is our little girl," said Papa, "but she's not so little any more. She's a young lady now. Turned thirteen last month."

Rose blushed at his words. She wasn't used to her new figure yet. She was filling out and growing taller and taller day by day. Sometimes she thought she was getting too tall. At five feet and four inches, she was already taller than her mother was.

"Well, Rose, I'm your Uncle Dermot and this is your Aunt Cora. And this is Bridget who is nearly your age. She's twelve."

"I'll be thirteen in three months," the girl announced assertively, almost before her father stopped speaking.

"Yes, she'll be thirteen in three months," Uncle Dermot repeated laughing, "and she'll never let us forget it. And this little one is our baby, Sean."

"Da, I'm not a baby. I'm four," Sean retorted.

Rose curtseyed. "I'm so happy to meet all of you."

After making arrangements for Rose's arrival in Utica and transfer to Aunt Jenny and Uncle Andrew's care, Papa hopped back onto the shore.

Rose felt her stomach tighten. She wanted to shout, Papa don't go. Don't leave me here with these people I don't know. But she said nothing and just waved. She brushed away the tears that started to fill her eyes and hoped no one saw them.

"Come here, child," said Aunt Cora. "Don't you worry. We'll take good care of you till you get to Utica. Right now Bridget will show you where to put your things."

"Come on. We need to go below." Bridget led the way to a set of stairs going down into the bottom of the cabin-like structure near the front of the boat.

Rose followed closely. "Why, this is just like a little house!" she exclaimed when they reached the bottom. To the right of her stood a wood stove for cooking and a table and chairs for eating. Above the table were plenty of shelves lined with an assortment of dishes, pots, and pans. Beef stew was cooking on the stove, filling the room with a delicious aroma. A newly baked apple pie was cooling on the table.

"Supper," said Bridget pointing to the stove. She paused and then continued, "That's where we do the cookin' and there's where we do learnin'." She pointed to a small high top desk to the left of them. "I don't much like cookin' but it's my job to help Mam with it." Alongside the desk was a curtained-off area containing bunks. "That's where the men sleep," Bridget added nodding in that direction. She then led Rose to another curtained area that opened into a kind of room. This was almost like a bedroom back home but instead of beds it had bunks. "The ladies sleep in here," she finished.

"This seems very cozy," said Rose. "But it's awfully warm down here. Is it always like that?"

"Usually. That's cuz of the stove. We need to keep a fire in it to cook, and some foods take a long time to cook like the stew. And before that we had to cook the pie."

"Oh," said Rose.

"I thought you had another brother," Rose began again, wondering where Tom was.

"Oh, I do," said Bridget laughing. "He's out tending the mules. He's our hoggee."

"What's a hoggee?" asked Rose puzzled.

"Don't you know anythin' about canal boats?" Bridget said impatiently. "A hoggee is a boy who walks alongside

13

The Finnegan Family

Uncle
Dermot

Aunt
Cora

Tom

Bridget

Sean

15

the mules and keeps them goin' on the towpath to pull the boat. Sometimes I have to help with that when Tom is tired, but most of all I help Mam with the cookin', washin', and household chores. I think Da is gonna hire another hoggee soon to help Tom out. That way Tom can help Da with the steerin' when Da is tired and also switch off walkin' the mules with the new hoggee. Hoggees usually take six hours on and six hours off to rest. It's tiresome doin' all that walkin'."

"They walk for six hours?"

"Sometimes they ride the mules part of the way, but they're not supposed to. Let's go on deck, so I can introduce you to Tom."

"Good idea," Rose said and lifted her long skirt to follow her cousin up the stairs. Bridget wore some kind of pants that looked like hand me downs from her brother, but seem more practical for travel on a boat. Rose had never seen a girl in pants before.

When they reached the top, Bridget called out to a tall, sandy-haired boy who turned and promptly ran toward the boat. He hopped on deck and stood facing the girls.

He was tall for fourteen, almost six feet, with his mother's hair and coloring. "Hello, you must be Rose," he said. "Pleased to meet you."

"Pleased to meet you too," said Rose awkwardly, shaking the hand he extended. He was very good looking, but he was her cousin.

"Gotta go back to the mules." And with that, Tom leaped onto the shore and was gone.

16

After a tasty supper, Aunt Cora suggested that Rose lie down for a while since she had had a very full day. Rose did not argue, as she did feel tuckered out. She went downstairs and slid onto the narrow bunk, resting her head on the tiny pillow. This was nothing like her bed at home.

Suddenly she heard water rushing forcefully under the boat. The noise kept getting louder and louder, and the boat began to rock from side to side.

"Help! Help! Aunt Cora, Uncle Dermot, the boat is sinking!" Rose ran into the kitchen area as fast as she could, her heart wildly beating away. Tears started to run down her cheeks.

"Man alive, the boat isn't sinkin'. Calm down," responded Bridget. "It's just goin' through a lock. Don't you know anythin'?"

"A lock? What's a lock?"

"Bridget don't be rude. Rose doesn't know about these things," said Aunt Cora, putting her arms around the shaking girl. "A lock is a water compartment, like a box, with gates at each end to raise or lower boats from one level of water to another. Right now we are going up, so water is coming in underneath to lift us. The gate will then open and let us out into the higher water."

The rushing sound stopped and all was quiet again. Rose breathed a sigh of relief. "Thank goodness that's over."

"It's not over," said Bridget. "We have to go through a lot more locks before we get to Schenectady. One right after another."

"Oh, no!" said Rose as the rushing sound started all over again, but now that she knew she wasn't in any danger, she could put up with it even though she didn't like it.

"Now that the dishes are done, why don't the two of you play checkers?" suggested Aunt Cora.

"Sure," said Bridget, "but no cryin' if you loose." She looked Rose in the eye.

Rose's face turned bright red.

"Bridget Finnegan! That was uncalled for! You apologize to your cousin right now."

"Oh, all right," said Bridget defiantly and then a tiny *sorry* escaped her lips.

"I…I…truly don't feel like playing checkers right now. I'm very tired and I just want to go to sleep." Rose felt like she had to get away from that girl immediately and pull herself together. "Goodnight."

She headed back into the sleeping room. Perhaps things would be better in the morning.

Chapter 3
Boat Life

Friday, August 7, 1840

I am writing this at the little desk in the kitchen area of the boat. I went to bed at nine last night and fell fast asleep the minute my head touched the pillow. I reckon I was exhausted from all that went on during the day. Thus, I awoke at six o' clock this morning and everyone else was still asleep. I ventured out here, so as not to wake them. I do not know when things get started around here, so hopefully I'll have time to write.

The Finnegans seem nice, except for Bridget. She is cruel and spiteful. I don't think I can ever be friends with someone like her and I was so wanting to. She is nothing like my friends Kathleen and Emma at school. They would never think of acting as she does.

I am much taller than Aunt Cora and Bridget, which makes me feel like a giant next to them. It's a good thing Uncle Dermot and Tom are taller than me.

I hope today will be better than yesterday. Going through the locks was a very upsetting experience. And Bridget wasn't very helpful. Oh, I wish I was home and not on this boat. I miss my family so much…

"Rose, what are you doing out here so early in the morning?" Aunt Cora parted the curtain and stepped into the room.

Rose jumped. "Oh, I was just writing in my journal." She quickly closed the book and replaced the quill in its holder.

"I'm sorry. I didn't mean to startle you. You can keep on writing."

"That's all right. I was just about finished."

"I got up to get breakfast started and noticed you were not in your bed, and I was wondering where you were."

"I reckon I went to bed so early last night I couldn't sleep anymore."

"Would you like to help me with breakfast?"

"Why, yes. I love to cook!"

Aunt Cora started the fire and then threw some more wood on it. While she and Rose were preparing the ham, eggs, fried potatoes, toast, and coffee, the rest of the family was beginning to stir and make their appearance in the kitchen.

"Smells awfully good out here," said Tom, buttoning up his shirt.

"Sure does," said Uncle Dermot, "but we need to eat quick and get the boat going.

"Here are your plates and coffee, all ready for you," said Aunt Cora.

"Hey, how come no one woke me up?" said Bridget as she wandered into the kitchen area with Sean. Seeing her mother and Rose cooking together made her feel left out.

"Rose helped me with the cooking, so I thought I'd let you sleep. I know how you hate to get up early," said Aunt Cora.

"Oh." That excuse didn't make Bridget feel any better.

After they ate, Tom was off to drive the mules, and Uncle Dermot went on deck to steer the boat. Rose and Bridget helped Aunt Cora with the dishes, and Sean played with his marbles in the corner of the room.

"I reckon Da will hire the new hoggee today when we get to the next town," said Aunt Cora.

"I hope he's good-looking," Bridget piped up.

Rose blushed. She was thinking that, too, but was not as bold as Bridget to say it out loud.

"Don't talk nonsense, Bridget. His job will be to work, not to entertain you," stated Aunt Cora. "Now, both of you gather up all the dirty clothing; today is wash day."

Aunt Cora put several pots of water on the stove to heat and a large bucket on the table to hold everything. First the water went in, then the dirty clothing, and last the

21

homemade soap. They showed Rose how to scrub each piece to remove the dirt and then to rinse it in the clean water.

"Where do you put these things to dry on a boat?" asked Rose as Bridget tossed the last piece into the basket.

"Come on, I'll show you," yelled Bridget as she ran upstairs with the laundry. Rose, Aunt Cora, and Sean followed behind.

"Is she always like this?" asked Rose.

"She's rather spirited, but she means well. You'll get used to her." Aunt Cora could tell that Rose was having a difficult time adjusting to Bridget's behavior.

On deck, Bridget had already started stringing a waist-high rope between two short poles along one side of the boat.

"Good work, Bridget. Let Rose give you a hand with that while I tie Sean to the rope."

"Why are you tying Sean to a rope?" Rose asked alarmed.

"That's so if he falls overboard we can quickly pull him up and he won't drown," said Aunt Cora. "It's hard to watch him when we're busy. Many a babe has died by falling into this canal." Her voice trembled at those words and she dabbed at her eyes with her apron. "I'm going down to fix lunch. You girls finish hanging the laundry and then you can rest for awhile."

When Aunt Cora was out of sight, Bridget whispered, "My baby sister, Mary, fell in and died when she was only two."

"How awful," said Rose. Now she understood.

"Mam still hasn't gotten over it. She doesn't like to talk about it."

"I see." Rose felt as though she had come upon a secret she was not supposed to know. "One more thing. Why is the clothes line so low?"

"That's because of the bridges. You sure ask a lot of questions," said Bridget.

"What bridges?" Rose smiled sheepishly. She just did it again.

"The low bridges. If the clothes are too high, the top of the bridge will knock them over. People have to duck when the boat goes under a low bridge, or they'll get knocked over, too."

"Do tell." Rose didn't know whether to believe Bridget or not since she liked to exaggerate things. "Are there a lot of bridges?"

"Yes. The canal goes through the middle of many of the farms along the canal and the farmers need a bridge to get from one side of their land to the other."

"Why did they build the bridges so low then?"

"It was cheaper that w...*duck,*" screamed Bridget.

Rose just stood there looking at her as though she was a crazy person.

Bridget pounced on Rose, knocking her to the floor and lay on top of her as the huge structure passed overhead.

"Get off of me!" Rose shrieked.

"Are you crazy? Do you wanna get killed?" Bridget yelled even louder. At that, she rolled off of Rose and they ended up sitting on the deck facing each other.

"*That* was the low bridge I was talkin' about," Bridget added.

"Ohhh…" Rose looked back and saw it. She felt about two inches tall. "Sorry. I thought you were trying to beat me up."

"I saved your life, cousin."

"Thank you, cousin." Maybe Bridget wasn't as bad as Rose thought she was. Maybe they could be friends.

After lunch, Rose decided to go out on the deck and take a look at the countryside. It was another beautiful day with the sun shining brightly. The banks of the canal were covered with lush greenery and all kinds of trees. Birds chirped their merry tunes. To her right was the towpath of worn gravel where the mules walked.

In some areas, there were stores and shops near the bank where you could purchase just about anything. Some shops even sent boats out to greet passersby to see if they needed anything and would actually bring the goods or food out to the customer. In other areas, there were houses, and people would wave as the boat went by.

There was something relaxing about gliding along at the slow pace of a canal boat. It wasn't scary at all like she thought it would be. She could even get to like this.

"Hello, cousin," said Bridget, interrupting her thoughts. "What are you doin' up here?"

"I just thought I'd look around at the canal. I didn't get a chance to see much of it yet."

"Do you want to play a game?" asked Bridget with a twinkle in her eyes.

"What kind of a game?" Rose wasn't sure she should trust her.

"Let's see who can stand the closest to the edge of the boat without falling off!"

"That's silly. Why would you want to do that?" Rose didn't like the sound of that game.

"Chicken! Balk...balk...balk!"

"Am not."

"Are, too. I can stand here, can you?" Bridget stood about two feet from the edge.

"Oh. I can stand a little closer." Before Rose knew it she was drawn in and participating, since she did not fear being a foot from the edge.

"I can get closer," sang Bridget as she shimmied past Rose to the edge.

"I give up. You win."

"*No*! I can stand on the edge. Look." And with that Bridget swayed back and forth and back and forth, shouting, "Yikes, help, help." Her foot slipped off the deck and she fell into the water screaming, "Help me, Rose, I'm drownin'," as her head went under a couple of times. And then all that was left was a tiny ripple where Bridget once was.

Rose ran with all her might into the cabin yelling, "Aunt Cora, Uncle Dermot, Bridget fell into the canal and is drowning. You've got to save her. Hurry!"

Aunt Cora looked up from her mending and said, "What's this nonsense, Rose? Bridget knows how to swim, and the canal is only four feet deep. She could stand up in it and so could you."

"But she fell in." Aunt Cora's words were not registering in her mind.

"I reckon she was trying to trick you. I'm going to have to have a talk with that girl."

Rose felt like the rug had been pulled out from under her. Her terror quickly turned to disgust. Bridget did it again. Could she ever trust her after this?

"Let's go and see what she's up to now," said Aunt Cora. She led the way up the stairs where they came upon a soaking wet Bridget, sitting on the deck laughing.

"That was not funny," Rose snapped.

"You've gone too far, young lady," said Aunt Cora. "You really frightened Rose with your antics. I think you need to spend the rest of the afternoon in the cabin. I'll be speaking to your father about what you did."

"It was just a joke," Bridget said as she got up and treaded wearily down the stairs.

"I'm sorry Bridget did that to you," said Aunt Cora. "She's always teasing and testing, I'm afraid. I hope she grows up soon."

Chapter 4
The New Hoggee

Friday, August 7, 1840
later

I just hate that Bridget! Every time I start to think that we are getting to be friends she does something terrible. Thank goodness for Aunt Cora. She is so kind and understanding. She let me help with the cooking and the washing and treats me like I was another daughter. If it weren't for her, I don't know if I could stand it another day on this boat. I reckon I will try to stay out of Bridget's way. Maybe then she'll leave me alone.

I miss my family and friends more than ever now and hope that Caleb is feeling better.

Uncle Dermot hired a new hoggee to help Tom when we passed through Schenectady. His name is Charles. He is fifteen years old and an orphan. There were a lot of boys looking for work, since being a hoggee pays ten dollars a month with meals and a place to sleep.

Uncle Dermot said he checked Charles out very carefully to make sure he was a good worker and an honest boy. I wonder how he can know that so soon. Charles seems to have passed the test because he is already out there on the towpath taking instructions from Tom.

Charles is almost six feet tall and has thick blonde hair that keeps falling into his eyes, which are the color of the sea. He is very handsome. Bridget was already making eyes at him when Uncle Dermot introduced him to us at supper.

We sure do eat well on the boat. Supper included ham, potatoes, green beans, homemade bread and butter, and spice cake for dessert. It was all very tasty. Aunt Cora is a great cook, almost as good as Mama.

This evening we are going to do some singing and dancing, and Uncle Dermot is going to play his fiddle and tell us stories. I reckon it will be an enjoyable evening.

Rose

Rose closed her journal and returned it to her hiding place under the pillow on her bunk in the sleeping room. One thing she did miss on the boat was her privacy. It seemed there was always someone around. She decided to start writing in the sleeping room during the daytime, so she could be alone.

Charles
The New Hoggee

"Rose, Rose, are you in there?" It was Bridget. "We are all ready on the deck for some fun. Mam sent me down to look for you, and Da is ready with the fiddle."

"I'm coming," said Rose as she followed Bridget towards the stairs.

"Isn't the new hoggee good-looking?" said Bridget.

"Oh, I reckon so." Rose blushed and was grateful for the darkness.

"He's sooo handsome. I hope he comes in for some time with us."

"Shhhh. You better not let your mother hear you talk like that."

The sight that greeted her when she came up on deck captivated Rose. Glowing oil lamps dimly lit the boat, revealing a table set with sweet treats, the deck swept clean, and everyone sitting on barrels ready to enjoy the evening. Crickets chirped, echoing back and forth across the canal. Fireflies flashed their lights on and off in the night sky. The mellow light made the canal look like a scene from a fairy tale.

Several boats were pulled up next to the *Flying Eagle,* and people moved from one to the other to join in the activities. Uncle Dermot had started playing his fiddle, and Aunt Cora was dancing with Sean.

Bridget headed over to the goodies table as soon as she spotted Charles there. He and Tom were sampling the cookies.

"Hello, Charles, are you having fun?" Bridget looked up into his eyes as she said it. He was even better looking close up.

"Yes, ma'am." Charles felt uncomfortable with her looking at him like that.

Tom laughed. "She's not a ma'am. She's my little sister. Just call her Bridget."

"I am *not* little," screeched Bridget. "Besides I'll be thirteen in three weeks." Why did people always have to bring up her size? She wished she were tall like Rose.

Just then a captain from another boat hopped onto the *Flying Eagle* with his harmonica and began to accompany Uncle Dermot, making the music even livelier.

"Do you want to dance, Charles?" Bridget asked.

"Me? Oh, no. I don't know how to dance, ma'am. I...I...mean Bridget."

"It's easy. I'll show you."

"Not right now. I'm tired from all that walking. I just want to sit and watch." Charles hoped she'd leave him alone. She certainly was bold.

"All right." She finally gave up on him and joined in dancing with the others on the boat.

Charles settled back into his former spot on the deck. He glanced around until his eyes rested on the other girl. *What was her name? Rose? That's right.* There was something about her that made him want to keep looking.

"Charles, let's go below and I'll show you where you sleep." Tom's voice interrupted his thoughts.

"Fine."

"I'm going to turn in now and you might want to, too. We need to be up mighty early tomorrow morning."

"I'm feeling mighty tired myself," said Charles.

"Why don't you boys take Sean down with you? It's way past his bedtime," stated Aunt Cora who was standing nearby.

The boys hoisted the child up onto their shoulders and carried him down the stairs into the cabin.

Shortly after, everyone else decided it was time to call it a day and departed for his or her own boat.

"Da, tell us a story before we go to bed," Bridget begged her father.

"It's too late."

"Just one."

"Oh, all right." Uncle Dermot couldn't resist his only daughter. "Did I ever tell you about my digging the canal?"

"Yes, just about 100 times," sighed Bridget.

"Yes, but Rose never heard it."

"Do you want to hear it, Rose?" asked Bridget.

"Why, yes I would." Rose knew a bit about the canal, but didn't know much about digging it.

"Well, it was 1819 when I came over from Ireland to work on the canal. There were too many people and too little opportunity to make a living in Ireland, so I thought I'd better leave and try my luck elsewhere. Everyone was saying that there were plenty of jobs with good hard cash, digging the canal in America. And they were right. I was young and strong and wanted to work, and work I did very hard. When the canal was done, I got a job as a hoggee. And I saved every penny I got from both jobs. As soon as I had enough money to send for my sisters, I brought them here, too."

"That would be my mother and Aunt Jenny," interrupted Rose.

"That's right, child," said Uncle Dermot. "Our parents didn't want to leave their home in Ireland and died in 1825 within a few months of each other from the consumption. Aye, it was too bad," he said as he wiped the corner of his eye with his handkerchief. "But… it was a long time ago, and I was happy to have Darcy and Jenny here. And do you know what? They came with a friend from the boat that they introduced to me. It was Cora, who became my wife a few months later."

Uncle Dermot reached up, grabbed Aunt Cora's arm, and pulled her onto his lap. "She's a good woman, my Cora."

"You're not so bad yourself, Dermot," said Aunt Cora, "but don't you think we should all be getting to bed now? Morning comes awfully soon."

"I have one more story for the girls before we turn in."

"Well, I'm going to bed. Goodnight! Don't keep them up too long," said Aunt Cora as she made her way down the stairs.

"This one's a ghost story," said Uncle Dermot.

"Oh, good," squealed Bridget, clapping her hands. She enjoyed the excitement that came with being scared.

Rose said nothing. She didn't reckon she was going to like this.

"Aghhhh." All of a sudden they heard a blood-curdling yell coming from the towpath.

Rose and Bridget were frozen in their spots.

"Wh-a-t was that?" Rose shuddered.

"I don't know. Da, what was it?" Bridget was beginning to feel a little jittery in spite of her usual boldness.

"Dunno," said Uncle Dermot wrinkling his brow. "Humm." He rose from his chair and cautiously walked to the edge of the deck to look around. "I don't see anything out there."

"Aghhhh." The horrible noise came again. This time it sounded louder and closer.

Rose and Bridget both screamed and grabbed onto each other for comfort.

"I know we should have gone to bed with Aunt Cora," whimpered Rose, feeling as if she was having a bad dream that she couldn't wake up from. Chills ran up and down her spine and goose bumps appeared on her arms.

Then something white darted out of the cabin stairwell and back into the shadows again. Now the dreadful sound came from there.

"There it is, Da. Get it," Bridget yelled.

Uncle Dermot ran after it, disappearing in the same place where the ghost had appeared. The girls were now alone. Their fears soared when he did not return.

"It probably killed him!" shrieked Bridget.

"Oh, no, there it is again!" Rose pointed her shaking finger towards the huge white shape with the awful moaning voice as it darted out again.

"I'll get it," murmured Bridget, grabbing her father's fiddle, trying to be courageous.

"*No*! Don't leave me here alone, please!" Rose had a death grip on her arm and wasn't about to let go.

"All right." Bridget just couldn't leave Rose, knowing the condition she was in. She wasn't too keen on fighting the ghost anyway. "Da. Da. Help us!" Bridget tried to summon her father.

The ghost appeared again and again and started coming closer and closer. The girls' eyes grew large as they peered at the intruder.

And then Bridget began to laugh.

Rose was startled at the change in her. How could her cousin laugh at a time like this? She was still shaking from head to toe.

"Tom!" yelled Bridget. She was now laughing hysterically.

"How did you figure that one out?" Tom said sheepishly as he tore the sheet from his head and then began to chuckle. Uncle Dermot followed behind, bellowing his hearty laugh.

The ghost appeared again and again and started
coming closer and closer...

"I recognized your shoes, stickin' out of the bottom of the sheet," said Bridget.

Rose immediately burst into tears. It was all too much for her.

"It was all a joke, Rose, laugh," yelled Bridget, tapping her on the back.

"Oh, only a joke." Rose feigned a smile, said, "Goodnight," in the calmest voice she could manage, and ran from the group. "It wasn't to me," Rose sobbed, wiping the tears that kept filling her eyes, wondering how they could be so cruel. She was still whimpering as she tried to settle down in her bunk for the night. *Those cousins sure have an odd sense of humor*, she thought, as she buried her face in her pillow and tried to muffle her cries so as not to wake the others. *My family would never do such things to each other. I wish I were home right now instead of on this boat.*

She was still awake when Bridget came in, but pretended to be asleep.

Chapter 5
Reading Lessons

Saturday, August 8, 1840

What a night! We had a wonderful time on the boat last evening with the singing and dancing. It was so much fun especially with the new hoggee there. Charles is so handsome, but I think Bridget likes him. She keeps looking at him and she asked him to dance. So I reckon I better not think about him too much, but I can still admire him from afar.

Then an awful thing happened that spoiled the whole evening. Tom decided to play a joke on us since he couldn't sleep. Being that Charles was here to help, Tom wasn't as tired as usual, so he got up and pretended to be a ghost to scare us. And was I scared. Uncle Dermot and Bridget just made light of it when they found out that the ghost was Tom, but I couldn't stop shaking and bawling. I am mortified that I acted like such a baby.

Aunt Cora was furious when she found out what they all did last night. Not only did she scold Tom and Bridget, she even gave Uncle Dermot a talking to. *I always feel better when I'm with her.*

Today I am going to sit in on Sean and Bridget's lessons. They cannot go to school when the boat is on the canal, so Aunt Cora teaches them. When the canal is closed from December to March, the family boards with Aunt Jenny, the children go to school in Utica, and Uncle Dermot works as a lumberjack. Bridget is lucky Uncle Dermot believes in education for girls, as many girls do not attend school at all. It must be hard to have friends under those conditions. I'm glad I attend the same school all the time.

Bridget says she doesn't like to read or do lessons, but Aunt Cora insists on it. Sean is just beginning to do letters and numbers.

I hope today is calm and peaceful.

Rose

Rose put the journal away and went into the kitchen area to help Aunt Cora and Bridget with the breakfast dishes. When they were finished, Aunt Cora fetched the Bible, slates, and chalk. Rose was sent to get Sean and returned with him in a few minutes.

"Let's start with reading, Bridget," said Aunt Cora as they gathered around the little desk, "and Sean can practice making his letters."

"Oh, no," said Bridget, "I hate readin'. I can never figure out all of those hard words."

"Now, Bridget, try. Read from the Bible on page 61 where we left off the last time."

Bridget opened the Bible and began to read. "The fam…fam…fame..."

"Famine," said Aunt Cora.

Bridget repeated it. "The famine was so sev…sev…" She stumbled again.

"Severe," said Aunt Cora. "Start over again, Bridget."

Rose was astonished at how poorly Bridget read. It was hard to listen to her.

"The famine was so severe that there was no food anywhere and the people of egg…egg..."

"That's Egypt." Aunt Cora seemed to have the patience of a saint.

"Wait, Aunt Cora, maybe I can help," said Rose. "Do you mind what Bridget uses for reading?"

"Why, no. But the Bible is the only book I have. Books are scarce."

"I have a book my Papa bought me called the McGuffey Reader. Usually they only have them in schools, but since Papa works for the paper, he was able to get one for me for my birthday. Would you like to try reading that one, Bridget?"

"No, I *hate* readin'," Bridget said forcefully.

"Wait till I get it. You might like this one," said Rose as she went behind the curtain and fetched the book from her bunk. She opened the book and read the last story to them. She just loved to read and it showed in the way she used expression and timing. It was like listening to a play.

"Rose, you are a wonderful reader!" said Aunt Cora.

Rose handed the book to Bridget. Bridget leafed through the pages and then opened it to the first page. "The words *do* look easier."

She read the first sentence and the next and then came to a word she didn't know. "Drat, I told you readin' is too hard. Don't you know anythin'?" She threw the book down and ran into the sleeping room.

"What good is readin'?" she yelled.

"Aunt Cora, I could help Bridget with her reading if you'd like me to," suggested Rose.

"Oh that would be wonderful," said Aunt Cora, "and I reckon you should use your book. It *is* easier." She stuck her head behind the curtain and called, "Bridget, come out here. Rose is going to help you with your reading."

Bridget emerged from the room at a snail's pace but agreed to the plan, thinking it would be easier to escape Rose than her mother if need be. The two girls went up on deck to get some fresh air while they finished the lesson. Aunt Cora worked with Sean below.

Rose remembered the way the teacher in school urged her to use the sounds of the letters to figure out words she didn't know. She explained the whole thing to Bridget, and after awhile, Bridget was beginning to notice some improvement in the way she was reading.

"Thank you, Rose. You're a good teacher," Bridget said when they were finished. "But I still don't know what *good* reading is," she screeched as she darted down the stairs. "Time to help Mam with supper."

Rose just shook her head in disbelief. "Poor Bridget," she said to herself.

Rose sat down on the deck to enjoy the scenery. Aunt Cora told her she could have some time off from cooking for helping Bridget. She was beginning to like the boat ride. They just seemed to slide over the water. The slow pace of two to four miles an hour was very relaxing.

Just as she was getting comfortable Charles leaped onto the deck from the towpath, his turn of walking was over. "Hello," he said, beaming from ear to ear as he neared her. "You're Rose, aren't you?"

"Yes," said Rose, jumping to a standing position. When her eyes met his, she felt heat rising in her cheeks and quickly looked away.

"So you're the cousin traveling with the cousins," he said continuing to grin. Suddenly a surge of energy seemed to replace his weariness.

"Yes, I'm going to Utica to help my Aunt Jenny out." She was glad he couldn't hear how fast her heart was beating.

"I was so fortunate to be hired by your uncle. Otherwise I'd still be on the streets of Schenectady looking for a place to sleep."

"Where are your parents?"

"They died in the cholera epidemic in '32 and I've been on my own almost since then."

"On your own? How awful! Don't you have any brothers or sisters?"

"Three brothers died in the epidemic, too. Only the baby and I survived. The neighbors took the baby and me in at first, but couldn't afford to keep me very long. They had five children of their own. And when I was eight, they thought I could make it on my own as a hoggee. So they contracted with a line boat friend of theirs to take me on and they let me go. I worked for that man for a few years, and then one winter the old man died, and come spring I found out that his wife sold the boat and went to live with her sister. From then on, I had to look for my own jobs."

"Oh, Charles," was all Rose could say. Her heart just ached for him.

"Don't feel sorry for me. I have a great job now and I'll be making good money and saving every bit of it until I have enough to buy my own boat like your Uncle Dermot. Then I'll be my own boss. Of course, I'd be willing to buy an old boat and fix her up, so it won't cost me the 3500 dollars for a new one." He felt at ease sharing his dreams with her even though he had just met her; she was such a good listener. It was a bit scary, but it felt good.

The boat swayed sharply to the left, nearly knocking them off of their feet. Charles grasped Rose by the arms to steady her. "Are you all right?" he asked as they straightened to a standing position.

Bridget appeared on deck at that very moment. "Hello, Charles, do you want...Oh, Rose, I didn't see *you* there."

Charles immediately let go of Rose's arms.

"What were you two doin' up here?" Bridget sounded annoyed.

"Just talking," said Charles.

"Can I talk, too?" Bridget added hopefully.

Charles suddenly felt exhaustion seeping through every part of his body, "I must go and sleep, now. It'll be my turn back on the towpath in six short hours. Goodbye, ladies."

"Wait," yelled Bridget. "Don't you wanna talk some more?" She asked almost pleadingly.

"Can't do it. Need to sleep. Maybe another time."

"See you later," said Rose while Bridget just sulked.

As soon as he left, Bridget put her hands on her hips, looked Rose angrily in the eyes, and said, "Rose, I told you I liked Charles. How come you were talkin' to him and he was holdin' your arms?"

"I didn't do anything. He started talking to me first when he got done with his turn on the towpath."

"Do tell," Bridget grumbled.

"Then the boat swerved and we nearly fell over and he helped me up."

"Pile on the agony." Bridget was furious. "Listen here, Rose. You better leave him alone." And with that she was gone.

Bridget stormed down into the kitchen area.

"I thought I told you to call Rose for supper," Aunt Cora said.

"I forgot. And anyway she can starve for all I care."

"What's the matter? Why are you so angry?"

"Rose and Charles were talkin' on the deck just now and when I came along and wanted to talk, Charles said he was tired and had to go." Bridget pouted.

"You'll have plenty of time to talk to Charles. He's here every day."

"But he doesn't want to talk to me. He only wants to talk to Rose."

"That's silly. You can all be friends."

"No, he likes Rose better than me. And I bet you do, too. Rose can cook better. Rose can read better. She even looks better than me," Bridget yelled out as she ran into the sleeping quarters and dropped onto her bed. She was *not* about to let herself cry.

"Bridget Finnegan, you come out here right now." Aunt Cora had heard enough.

A fuming Bridget emerged and faced her mother.

"What is all this nonsense? You know I love you very much. You're my child. Sometimes you can be pretty difficult, but I do love you. How can you doubt that?" Aunt Cora's voice began sharply but then softened a bit. She held out her arms to Bridget. "Oh, Bridget, you're my little girl."

Bridget went over and let her mother hug her. She felt a bit better, but still did not like the idea of Charles talking to Rose.

Chapter 6
Fire! Fire!

Saturday, August 8, 1840
later

Well, we are almost to Utica. We should be there tomorrow at candle lighting time or early the next day, so says Uncle Dermot.

Bridget is angry with me again. It seems everything I do annoys her. All I did was talk to Charles this time.

Charles is a very remarkable boy for his age. He has great plans for the future already. I reckon Uncle Dermot was right when he said he was a good worker and an honest boy. He keeps stopping me to talk whenever he's on deck. He told me all about his family, and how he became an orphan. It is so sad.

After a supper of stewed beef with gravy, mashed potatoes, corn dripping with butter, homemade rolls, and pound cake for dessert, tonight was just for playing games and really telling stories. We played checkers and Bridget beat me four out of five times. She was happy about that.

Tom beat me once and I beat Sean two times. I am not very good at checkers.

Then Uncle Dermot told us a ghost story about the Montezuma Swamp. It was all about canawlers going by there, hearing dreadful sounds coming from it at night. One day a man decided to go in to see what was making such a racket, and he was never heard from again. Then another man decided to go in, and when he came back, he had no legs. A third man came back with no arms. A fourth one had no head. The last man that went in came back a ghost. And now the boat is called the Ghost Ship and still goes up and down the canal at night, scaring all the people on the other boats. When Uncle Dermot got through, I felt like I might jump right out of my skin I was so scared.

Aunt Cora surprised us later with warm vanilla and chocolate taffy she had made while we were listening to the stories, and we had taffy pull. It was so much fun. Even Charles couldn't bear to leave and stayed for an hour of his usual sleeping time.

I hope I never see the Ghost Ship.

Rose

Rose heard familiar voices in the other room when she awoke the next morning.

"Goodmornin' Charles," she heard Bridget say.

"Oh, hello. What are you doing up so early?" He responded, slipping on his boot.

"Gettin' breakfast started for Mam. She's helpin' Da with a boat repair, and Tom's already out there with the mules."

"Well, I better get out there and give them a hand," said Charles, putting the other boot on.

Rose stuck her head out of the curtain. "Need some help, Bridget?"

"Sure do."

"Here I am," Rose said as she entered the room. Her hair was neatly braided into two pigtails, and she wore a sky blue dress that mirrored the color of her eyes.

Charles let out a long, low whistle. "Hello, Rose. You sure look good in the morning."

Bridget just rolled her eyes.

"Hello," Rose managed to say, but she could feel her face get hot and turned away, so the others could not see it. She just hated that revealing blush. Why did it have to happen?

"What's the matter?" asked Charles grabbing her by the shoulders and turning her around until she faced him.

"Nothing," said Rose trying not to meet his eyes.

"Nothin' is wrong, Charles, but you need to get out there and help Da." In her attempt to divert his attention, Bridget unknowingly saved the day for Rose.

"Oh, I thought I did something wrong. I guess I *should* go out there and help." With that Charles was gone.

"Thank you, Bridget." Rose was relieved.

"I didn't do anythin'."

"Never mind. Let's start cooking," said Rose.

Bridget was happy that Rose changed the subject. She felt guilty, having purposely sent Charles away, so he couldn't pay attention to Rose.

"All right, you get the eggs goin' and I'll start fryin' the ham," said Bridget, sounding like a general barking out orders.

Rose greased the pan with butter, cracked a half a dozen eggs into it, and set it on the stove to cook. Meanwhile, she started setting the table with the pretty morning glory china that had been one of Aunt Cora's wedding presents.

Bridget was trying to hurry the ham by stoking the fire. The large amount of wood she had added to it earlier ended up creating a hot blaze. As she poked at it, flames began to shoot out of the stove, catching the pan on fire.

"Help, Rose!" Bridget screamed while she tried to move the pan. "Get the bucket of water."

All Rose could do was stare. She was frozen to the spot with fear.

"Rose!" Bridget screamed again. By now the pan with the eggs was also on fire.

Finally able to move, Rose ran over to the fire and began trying to blow it out. The flame only grew larger, and soon her pigtail ribbon caught on fire and started to burn. She yelped.

Bridget dropped the poker, bent down, and picked the buckets up herself, soaking Rose with the first one and the stove with the next two. Good thing her mother insisted on having water near the stove.

"There, it's out," said Bridget. "Why did you blow on the fire? You almost got us killed! Don't you know anythin'?" She was furious.

"I'm sorry. I didn't know that would make it worse." Rose was now crying.

"Oh, I'm sorry, too, for yellin' at you." Bridget sensed herself softening. She felt sorry for Rose. She always seemed to be crying. "The important thing is that the fire is out and we're both safe."

"Thank you for saving me again." Rose hugged Bridget. "I owe my life to you, so don't you think we can be friends now?" She felt very generous. "I can put up with your jokes if you can have some patience with a newcomer."

"Oh, all right," Bridget laughed, feeling silly, "I'll try."

They both hugged again. Rose changed her clothes, and then they got to work, cleaning up the mess in the kitchen.

The rest of the family returned to what they thought would be breakfast waiting for them only to be shocked by the horrible mess in the kitchen.

When she heard what had happened, Aunt Cora hugged both of the girls, said she was thankful they were safe, and then got busy helping them to clean things up. The men had to be satisfied with cold buttered bread, apples, and milk for breakfast since the fire was out, and the stove was so wet it would take forever to be able to restart it.

"Everybody jump," yelled Bridget as the boat neared the shore.

Aunt Cora decided that she, Rose, and Bridget would stop at a canal-side store to pick up some groceries and supplies while the boat was waiting to go through a lock. There were several boats waiting for their turn, causing a travel delay. They would have plenty of time to shop.

"We just have to get some of those delicious blackberries," said Aunt Cora handing a bucket of them to Rose. "You hold on to these so they won't get crushed."

"We can make a blackberry cobbler," said Rose.

"Good idea. We also need some meat and flour right here," Aunt Cora continued, putting those things into the cloth bag she brought with her. "Let's get some of these nice, fresh green beans, too."

"Da said he needed some new towline rope and oil for the lamp," Bridget reminded her.

"Oh, yes. You go look for them, and we'll meet you in the front of the store." Aunt Cora added some pickles from the large crock as a special treat for Sean and the men, and then she was done.

When the purchases were made, they returned to the boat and found that it had still not gone through the lock. Aunt Cora asked Rose to help her with the cobbler, whereas Bridget was sent up to watch Sean as he played on deck.

"Aunt Cora, what's wrong with me?" Rose asked as she mixed the ingredients for the dough. "Just when I think I'm getting used to everything on this boat, something new happens and I feel jumpy again." Rose hoped Aunt Cora could be as helpful as her mother was when she had a problem.

"I'll tell you what's wrong with you Rose Stewart!" Bridget's voice startled them. "You're just too scared. Too scared of everythin'." She had returned to get a sweater for Sean and had overheard them. "I can tell you how to change," she added.

"Bridget!" Aunt Cora's tone of voice revealed her disapproval.

Bridget ran up the stairs and onto the deck.

The endless fear returned to Rose's eyes. Her stomach began to tighten.

"Rose, you're just a sensitive person. You and Bridget are very different."

"I know, but I wish I could be more like her."

Aunt Cora laughed. "I don't think so. Look at all the trouble she gets into."

"But she has such fun."

"I bet she wishes she was a little more like you. Ever since you came on the boat, she's started combing her hair more often and wearing her nicer clothes."

"Me?" It was Rose's turn to laugh then.

"Dermot and I have lived on this boat since our marriage. Bridget and the boys were born on it. They have learned to accept new people, places, and things. It's the only way to survive the travel we always do and be happy. You've been brought up in one town with the same neighbors and friends. You'll change as you grow older and experience more new things and meet new people. It just takes time."

"I reckon so," said Rose feeling a little better.

They continued chatting while they finished making the cobbler.

Then Rose decided to go up on deck to look for Bridget. She found her trying to draw a picture of Charles which she immediately hid behind her back.

"Bridget, what did you mean when you said you knew how I could change?"

"Oh, nothin'. Sometimes I talk too much."

"No, I really want to know."

"Well... know how you're scared all the time."

"Yes."

"Well, you just have to do the thing you're scared of, and the more you do that the less scared you'll be."

"Do tell," said Rose.

"Yes, that's what I do." Bridget put her hand to her mouth. She hadn't meant to say that.

"*You* get scared?" Rose was surprised.

"Everyone gets scared sometimes," Bridget admitted. "Don't you know anythin'?" She scolded. "Sometimes gettin' scared can be excitin', too!"

"Exciting?" Rose couldn't believe what she was hearing. "What do you mean by that?"

"Like when you're listenin' to scary stories and your heart starts a racin' and you can feel the blood rush to your head. It's kind of excitin'!"

"Oh," Rose said. But she wondered how anyone in their right mind could think that being scared was exciting.

Chapter 7
Calamity on the Boat

Sunday, August 9, 1840

Now that the trip is almost over, Bridget has decided we can be friends. She said she thought I was the one who didn't like her because I acted kind of uppity, and all along I thought she didn't want to be friends with me.

I am like that. Sometimes I think too much and don't do much talking. People think I'm stuck up, but I'm just shy. I'm not very outgoing.

Bridget told me something I'm going to try to remember: When you're scared, just do the thing you're scared of, and the more you do that the less scared you'll be. I am going to try that to see if it works. After our talk last night, Bridget said she was going to try to be more careful about what she says to people. I'll believe it when I see it.

We attended church this morning. It was different from any other church I ever went to. It was a church on a boat called a gospel boat especially for canawlers and canal side families. These people preach from the Bible on the deck of the boat. Aunt Cora says if we can't go to church on land, the church will come to us. She was right.

I've been helping Bridget with her reading, as much as I can, and she seems to be doing much better with it. Aunt Cora sure is happy about that.

I wonder how Caleb is doing. I hope his leg is better now. It's been three days since I left on this trip, and I still miss Mama, Papa, and the rest of my family very much.

I am going to miss Aunt Cora when I get to Utica. She has been like a second mother to me. I hope Aunt Jenny is as nice as she is. But I'm not going to worry about it!!

Rose

"Ohhhh," Bridget moaned as she pushed through the curtain and dropped onto her bed.

"What's the matter?" asked Rose. She had just finished tucking her journal under her pillow.

"Ohhhh, I don't feel so good." Bridget's face looked awfully pale. "Mam told me to lie down for awhile to see if I get over it."

"Get over what?" Rose hoped she wasn't getting the cholera.

"The taffy."

"The taffy?"

"I found the extra taffy Mam hid and I ate it all."

58

"Oh, no! And now you're sick."

"That I am. That I am." Bridget moaned again. "You'll have to help Mam until I get better.

"Sure. I'll go out right now and let you rest." Rose rolled her eyes. That Bridget. She sure could get in trouble.

Aunt Cora was almost finished making lunch when Rose emerged from the sleeping area.

"What can I do to help?" Rose asked.

"I'm all caught up here with the cooking. Lunch will be ready in about half an hour, so could you tell Uncle Dermot and Charles that? Tom is still sleeping, so I'll wake him when it's done. He can eat first and then switch with Charles for his turn on the towpath. I reckon Bridget won't be eating for awhile."

"I reckon not. All right, I'll be back soon." Rose headed up the stairs and gave Uncle Dermot the message first since he was on deck steering, and then hopped onto the towpath to inform Charles.

She felt the uneasiness creeping in just at the thought of speaking to Charles. How she *hated* being shy. But wait. What did Bridget say? *When you're scared, just do the thing you're scared of, and the more you do that the less scared you'll be.* She would try it.

"Charles," she called out as she walked toward him, still feeling anxious.

"Hello, Rose. What are you doing out here?" He pushed a lock of his thick blond hair out of his eyes.

"Aunt Cora asked me to tell you lunch would be ready in half an hour, so you can come in then."

"Fine. So your aunt tells me you're quite a good reader. Says you helped Bridget learn to read better."

"Oh, yes, I love to read."

"I don't know how to read, myself," he hesitated, "but I want to learn. I think it's important to know how."

Rose could hardly believe her ears. He was fifteen years old and didn't even know how to read.

"I never did have much schooling, being on my own and all, and before that I had to help my Pa on the farm."

"I have some books. If I was going to be on the boat longer, I could help you learn," Rose remarked, surprising herself by her response. He was so easy to talk to.

"You would do that for me? You hardly even know me." He smiled at her. She certainly was generous.

"Maybe if you're still here on the trip back, I could do it then," she said, smiling back.

"I'll be here. Your Uncle is a good boss. Some of the captains do not treat hoggees very well. They cheat them and overwork them. I was on a couple of boats like that for awhile."

"What happened?"

"I ran away. More than once. I never want to work for a boss like that again." He shuddered a little when he said that. "What about you, Rose? How long will you be in Utica?"

60

"I'll be there for three weeks. Then I'll be going back home to Albany on Uncle Dermot's boat," Rose responded.

"Good. Then I'll get to see you again." His words made her blush.

"And, I can help you with your reading then," she said quickly, hoping he didn't see the redness.

"It's a deal." He felt like he wanted to keep talking to her. "So what do you like to do besides reading?" he added.

"Oh, I like to write in my journal and cook and I love history. My Papa tells me a lot of stories about what happened in the past." Her voice quickened and rose with excitement as she went on, "Like when the Erie Canal was first built and the opening ceremony."

"Do tell," he said.

"Rose, Charles, where are you? Lunch is ready," Aunt Cora shouted from the boat.

"Oh, no! I stayed too long," Rose gasped. "I was supposed to call you in."

"We're coming," Charles answered for both of them. Then he turned to Rose and said, "That's all right, I really enjoyed your company. It gets lonely out here all by myself." Rose sure was an interesting girl and very thoughtful.

Rose felt happy all over. *Maybe Bridget was right. Maybe you just have to do the thing you're scared of,* she thought.

Then they went in for lunch.

"The sky sure is getting dark out there," said Uncle Dermot when he came in for a glass of water. "It's only three o'clock and it already looks like evening. I think we're in for a big storm."

"I know," Aunt Cora said. "I had to light the oil lamp, so we could see what we're doing." She and Rose were knitting in the kitchen area while supper simmered on the back burner of the stove. Sean was playing with his marbles on the floor.

"How's Bridget feeling?" Uncle Dermot asked.

"She'll be fine once she gives her stomach a rest," said Aunt Cora.

"I need to get back up there to keep an eye on the weather." Uncle Dermot downed the drink quickly and rushed out of the cabin.

It grew darker and darker outside.

Bridget poked her head out of the curtain. "Is it night already? How long did I sleep?"

"It's afternoon, but there's a big storm coming," said Aunt Cora.

"Oh, good!" Bridget exclaimed. "I hope there's a lot of thunder and lightnin'."

Rose paled when she heard that. She hated thunder and lightning.

"I take it you feel better now," Aunt Cora said to Bridget.

"Oh, yes, now I'm hungry," stated Bridget.

"There are some leftovers on the table but don't eat too much. It'll be suppertime soon."

Then the rain came. First little sprinkles hit the outside of the boat. Then giant powerful drops pelted it from all directions. The wind picked up and whistled through the windows. Huge streaks of lightning lit up the inside of the cabin. Roaring claps of thunder followed closely behind.

Rose dropped her knitting and put her hands over her ears. Her eyes were as big as saucers. "How long do you reckon this will last?" she whispered nervously.

Bridget jumped up and ran to the window for a better look. "A long time, I hope. This is fun."

"I'm scared," Sean wailed and rushed over to his mother's side.

"There, there, little one. The storm will be over before you know it. We just have to wait it out. Stay with Mam." She picked him up and put him on her lap, holding him close. He buried his head deep in her shoulder and covered his ears with his hands.

Uncle Dermot and Tom came running in from the deck.

"I've secured the boat and Tom took care of the mules. We have to stop till this is over. It's too bad out there," said Uncle Dermot.

Charles, startled by the noise, awoke instantly and rolled out of his bunk onto the cabin floor. "What's all the racket?" he asked as he quickly scrambled to his feet.

"A bad storm," said Tom.

"I'll say," said Charles still not fully awake.

Rain continued to beat down on the boat. Even though it was tied down, it swayed back and forth. It felt like an enormous rocking horse. When the wind shifted, the boat also bobbed up and down.

Rose was back to disliking boats again. She was beginning to feel sick.

"Come here, Rose, look at the lightnin'. It looks like streaks in the sky when it flashes." Bridget stood at the window with the curtain drawn back so she could see better. She was captivated by the display.

Rose shuddered. *Do the thing you're scared of,* was all she could remember of what Bridget had told her. She slowly walked toward the window, telling herself over and over that she wasn't afraid. But when she reached the sill, an enormous bolt hit. It looked as though it had cut the sky in two. It was followed by the loudest noise Rose had ever heard. She clapped her hands over her ears and ran in the opposite direction sobbing with all her might. She had to get away from there.

Before she knew what she was doing, she had run up the stairs and was on the deck. Rain was coming down all around, soaking her to the skin. Her long dress, wet and heavy now, stuck to her legs. Her feet slipped on the soggy deck leaving her lying there helpless. She was frozen with fear as lightning struck again and again. It felt like the end of the world to her.

"Rose, come back," the others yelled.

"I'll go get her," Uncle Dermot shouted as he donned his raincoat and ran up after her. "Rose, you went the wrong way," he yelled when he saw her. "You don't want to be out here when it's like this. It's dangerous! Crawl over here and give me your hand. I'll help you in."

He soon realized that Rose, not thinking rationally at the moment, was unable to move. He slowly inched his way across the slippery deck, lifted her up, and carried her down the stairs to safety.

Even after she was inside, Rose could not stop weeping. She felt like such a fool, endangering herself and her uncle.

Aunt Cora wrapped her in a blanket and led her into the sleeping quarters. "There, there, you'll be all right, child," she said. "You're safe now."

"Aunt Cora, I tried what Bridget told me to do," Rose said between sobs, "but it didn't work. I was still scared of the lightning."

"What did Bridget say?" Aunt Cora asked suspiciously.

"She said to do the thing you're scared of and the more you do it the less scared you'll be. It worked the first time I tried it but not this time." The tears were beginning to slow down.

"That *is* a very good plan. I'm surprised that Bridget thought of it. But you know, Rose, you can't change overnight. It takes time. Maybe it won't work all the time, but the important thing is that you are trying, and the more you try the more successful you'll be."

"Do tell. Then I reckon I'll just have to keep trying," Rose said as she hugged her aunt. "I always feel so much better when I talk to you. I love you, Aunt Cora."

Chapter 8
A Setback

Today was my worst day ever on the boat. We had a very bad storm in the late afternoon. I tried to be daring and enjoy the lightning like Bridget does, but I ended up in a fright and cried like a baby once more. Just thinking about it gives me goose bumps and a weak stomach all over again. I wish I were braver.

Uncle Dermot and the other men alerted a runner to Utica that we would be a day late getting in. The storm's wind and rain caused the canal bank ahead of us to wash out. A hurry up-boat came quickly, and the men are still working to repair the break. That is a special kind of boat that rushes to the scene of an emergency and fixes it. Many boats all around us are waiting, as we are, to continue their journeys. Bridget says it takes awhile for them to build up the bank. Then we will have to wait until it is our turn to leave.

Bridget was displeased with me when she found out that Charles talked to me on the towpath. I tried to tell her that I could not be bad mannered and ignore him if he talked to me first. But she would not listen. She did not stay angry very long and came back to talk a while later. She asked me why Charles talks to me more than to her. I told her maybe it was because of the way she says things. She said she's going to try to be a little more careful from now on. I reckon we both have problems but they're different. I didn't think anything ever bothered her. I'm starting to like her a little now. Maybe we can be friends after all.

I reckon we will have one more day on the boat. So, I might as well go to sleep now. I think I've had enough excitement for one day.

I hope Caleb is better and everything is all right at home.

Rose

Although she fell asleep quickly, Rose kept tossing about, dreaming she was still out in the storm. Each time she awoke petrified, she had to remind herself that it was over and she was safe. She finally fell into a deep sleep only to be roused by Bridget's voice.

"Rose, Rose, wake up! We're finally movin'!"

"Oh…good." Rose rubbed her eyes and pulled the blanket over her head. "What time is it?" she murmured.

"Eight o'clock. We let you sleep late cuz we knew you were tired."

"Eight o'clock?" Rose yanked back the covers and jumped up startled. "I have to help with breakfast."

"No, silly. We already ate. Yours is on the stove."

"Oh." Rose dropped back onto the bunk. She was still tired.

"Da says we should be in Utica this evenin'. The men worked all night and finally fixed the wash out. Isn't that great news?"

"It sure is." Rose suddenly felt more energetic. "I have to get up and get dressed."

"Oh, there's one little problem," said Bridget, "you know that carpetbag you have your clothes in. Well, it was up on deck under the awnin', and when it stormed so hard, the rain blew right in sideways and all of your clothes are wet."

"Oh, no! What am I going to wear? The clothes I had on last night are all wet, too."

"Mam and I hung your clothes out to dry on a line on the deck. They should be ready soon. She said you're to wear some of Tom's old ones. Here." Bridget held out a pair of faded blue pants and an old white shirt. "I'll wait in the other room while you change."

"You want me to wear *that*?"

"Just till your clothes dry."

"No, I can't wear boy's clothes," said Rose.

"Fine. Then you'll have to walk around in your nightdress. Don't you know anythin'?"

"That's even worse." Rose realized she didn't have much of a choice. She either had to wear those clothes, or stay in the sleeping quarters all day. "Fine!" She finally gave in grudgingly. After all Bridget wore pants much of the time, and she seemed to like them. Rose felt strange putting them on and even more uncomfortable when she was ready.

Bridget took one look at her when she emerged from the sleeping area and began laughing uncontrollably. She covered her mouth with her hands to try to hold back the outburst, but it was no use.

"It's not funny, Bridget," said Rose crossly.

"Is, too."

Rose took one look at herself in the mirror and then she began to chuckle, too. She certainly did look funny. They both laughed so hard they ended up on the floor, holding their sides.

"What's going on down there?" asked Aunt Cora from the stairway.

"Nothin'. Rose is gettin' dressed," said Bridget.

"I just came down to see if you were all right," she said, turning to Rose. "You had quite a scare last night."

"I'm fine," Rose said scrambling to her feet.

"It's about time you two girls got to be friends. It's a shame. Four days together and you just couldn't get along." Aunt Cora shook her head as she headed up the stairs to the deck.

"I didn't think you wanted to be my friend," they both said together and broke out laughing again.

"If truth be told," said Rose, "you played all those tricks on me and said some mean things, too."

"Oh, I was just havin' some fun. Don't you like to have fun? And the other is just the way I talk."

"I reckon I'm just not used to having *that* kind of fun."

"And you were so high and mighty and snooty when you got on the boat. You didn't even talk to me. You just kept writin' in that book. I didn't reckon you were interested in havin' a friend."

Rose twisted a strand of her dark hair around her finger. "Oh, I just feel uneasy around new people. I wish I wasn't so shy," she said. But she didn't tell Bridget that she really didn't like her at first.

"Let's go up on deck and play checkers," said Bridget. "We only have this one day left to be friends."

"No we don't. I'll be going back to Albany on the boat when I'm done helping Aunt Jenny."

"That's true. Beat you up the stairs." Bridget turned and ran.

I guess Bridget will be Bridget, Rose thought as she followed her up, *I hope she doesn't beat me in every game this time.*

Outside the sky was clear and bright blue. The air smelled as though everything had been given a washing. It was a pleasure to be on the deck now with the sun shining rather than last night in the storm.

The girls settled down in one corner of the boat to play their game. Bridget won the first three games, and just

71

when Rose was about to give up, she finally won one. She also won the next one much to Bridget's surprise.

"Now, Rose, when did you get to be such a good checker player?" Bridget asked scratching her head. "You're not supposed to beat me!"

"I learned from you," said Rose laughing. "Do you want to stop playing now?"

"No, let's just play one more."

"All right."

Bridget had her revenge and won the last game. It really didn't matter that much to Rose. She enjoyed playing just as much as winning.

"Are you girls going to help me with lunch, or are you going to play all day?" Aunt Cora yelled from downstairs.

"Coming," they both shouted at once.

"Beat you down," yelled Bridget leaving Rose to pick up the checker game and put it away.

When Rose finally got downstairs, Aunt Cora had already started preparing the apple crisp and was taking freshly baked bread out of the oven. Bridget was peeling potatoes. "What took you so long?" she teased.

"I had to put *your* checker game away. You left it right in the middle of the deck," Rose stated, giving Bridget a disapproving look.

"Oh, I forgot... I'm sorry Rose. You'll forgive me, won't you?" Bridget sounded quite sincere.

"Bridget," said Aunt Cora, "you always seem to forget the things you don't want to do."

"I know," Bridget said putting her hand over the laugh that was about to escape from her mouth.

Then they all had a good laugh... Bridget, Rose, and Aunt Cora.

In one hour, lunch was ready and the men were called. Steaming mashed potatoes, sour crout, pickles, and fried ham awaited them, along with the bread and apple crisp the women had made earlier.

Uncle Dermot said grace and ate first with the women and Sean. Tom and Charles would take turns when he was through, as the boys were needed to keep the boat going.

"Who is this new boy?" Charles teased when he came in for lunch. He slid into the seat next to Rose who was finishing her apple crisp.

Rose could feel her cheeks get warm. She didn't know what to say and didn't want Charles seeing her in boy's clothes.

"It's just us," said Bridget.

"Rose's clothes got wet in the storm, so this is all she has," Aunt Cora explained.

"Well, do you know what? You still look pretty even in those clothes," Charles whispered, giving her an admiring glance.

Rose's face turned beet red at that, and she wanted to run away so he wouldn't see it, but Bridget's advice flashed through her mind before she could make a move. *The more you do the thing you're scared of the less scared you'll be.* And she decided, at that very moment, that she would stay there and talk to everyone no matter how uncomfortable she felt.

"Charles, can I help you with the mules this afternoon?" Bridget asked boldly.

Before he had a chance to answer her, Aunt Cora intervened. "No, you may not young lady. I need you here to help me with the jam. I need to make jam from the rest of the blackberries before we get to Utica or they will spoil."

As the conversation proceeded, Rose felt herself relax and as she did, the flush began to leave her face. "Can I help, too?" she asked.

"I was counting on it. I'm going to need both of you girls to take turns cooking and taking care of Sean."

All the while they were sitting there, Charles kept stealing glances at Rose. "Well, I'd better get back to the mules so Tom can eat," he said reluctantly, making his way to the stairs. "Rose, can I talk to you for a minute?"

"Sure," she said following him to the doorway.

"Listen, do you think you could get away to the towpath this afternoon. I want to talk to you before you leave."

"I'll try," she said.

Chapter 9
The Talk

I am writing this after lunch in the sleeping room. Everyone is busy doing something else right now, so I have the room to myself. Soon I need to help Aunt Cora with the blackberry jam.

Charles saw me in Tom's clothes. I was so embarrassed. Then he said I looked pretty, and that awful heat and redness filled my cheeks, and I almost dashed out of the room, so he would not see it. Why do I have to be so bashful? I think he is very handsome and I think he likes me. He wants me to meet him on the towpath this afternoon. I will try to get away when the jam making is done. I hope Bridget doesn't get mad at me for talking to him.

Bridget and I had a good time today playing checkers and fixing lunch. She seems to be friendlier to me now. I can't believe she wanted to be friends with me all the while; she didn't act like it. She is trying to be agreeable

*and to remember to think before she does something.
Sometimes it works and sometimes it doesn't. But at least
she is trying.*

*I am making an effort to take Bridget's advice about
trying to be less afraid of things and to have more fun. I
find it difficult, but it's becoming a little easier as I keep
doing it. I'm trying to laugh when Bridget laughs and not
to take her jokes so seriously.*

*Tonight we arrive in Utica, at last. I look forward to
meeting my Aunt Jenny and her family. But I am nervous
too. Because I must meet new people all over again and
get to know them. And I miss my family. I wish Mama
were here with me. It would make it so much easier. It
seems so long since I've seen them and yet it's only been
four days.*

Now I must go and help Aunt Cora with the jam.

Rose

Rose tucked her diary under her pillow and stepped out
into the eating area. Aunt Cora had already filled a huge
pot with water for cleaning the blackberries. The table was
covered with old papers while sparkling clean, small
crocks were lined up like soldiers on one end of it.

Aunt Cora dropped about half of the berries into the
water, skimmed any debris off the top, pulled them out
with a large slotted spoon, and had Bridget mash them one
layer at a time in a large stock pot. Rose was told to add

the sugar to the pot when the berries came to a boil, and to stir it all in. Then the mixture was boiled for about a half hour until it began to jell. Aunt Cora showed Rose how to let the mixture run off of a spoon to test for doneness.

When it was ready, Aunt Cora carefully poured the jam into the crocks. "The foam on top will keep the jam from spoiling," she said.

This process was repeated once more, and then they were finally done.

"You go on and start getting your things together, Rose, so you'll be all ready when we get to Utica. Bridget can help me clean up here," said Aunt Cora.

"Are you sure?" Rose asked. All Rose had been think about was seeing Charles on the towpath and what he could possibly want to talk to her about. She had been wondering how she was going to get away without Bridget noticing it. Now she had the perfect chance.

She remembered that she still had Tom's old clothes on and decided to change into some of her own that were finally dry. She put on her sky blue dress, the one that made her eyes look like sapphires, and arranged her long dark hair attractively around her face. Then she slipped up to the deck without anyone noticing it.

Charles was on the towpath driving the mules. Rose lifted her long skirt, jumped the short span from the boat to the shore, and walked towards him.

"Charles." Her heart beat faster as she nervously called his name. "Did you say you wanted to talk to me?"

"Yes, Rose." He turned to look at her. "I want to ask you for a favor. You know how good you are at reading and that I can't read."

"Yes," said Rose.

"Well, I have this letter and I was wondering if you could read it for me. It's a letter my mother wrote to me before she passed away. I didn't know anyone well enough to ask them to read it to me before, so I've carried it around with me all this time. You were so nice and friendly the last time we talked that I thought maybe you wouldn't mind reading it to me. What do you think?" He looked worried as though he might be asking too much of her.

"Of course, I can read it to you." Rose felt sad for him, losing his family at such a young age. She didn't know what she'd do without Mama, Papa, and her brothers and sister.

Charles took an envelope out of his pocket and handed it to Rose.

She opened the yellowed paper carefully and read:

To my wonderful son Charles,
    I know I will not be on this earth very much longer. I grow weaker and sicker by the hour. Already your father and brothers are with the Lord, and I will soon be joining them.
    I have made arrangements for the neighbors to take you and Susan after I am gone. I hope they are good to you.

"Well, I have this letter and I was wondering if you could read it for me," asked Charles.

I just want you to know that your father and I loved you very much. You were our first-born. You were such a beautiful baby and brought such joy into our lives. It was as though God took a little bit of the best parts of each of us and put them in you. And when you started growing up you were a wonderful child. You were kind and thoughtful and very considerate of others. You helped take care of your sister and brothers and never complained about it.

Rose's eyes were wet as she read on. She tried to keep her voice steady:

Some day you will be a man. I won't be there to see it, but I hope you remember us and the life we shared in the little cabin. I hope someday you will marry and have a family of your own and that nothing but good happens to you.
I love you.

Your mother,
Anna Williams

Charles now had his back to her, and when Rose went around to face him, she saw that he too had tears in his eyes. "I never knew she thought those things about me," he said awkwardly.

"Oh, Charles, that is such a beautiful letter," cried Rose. "Your mother must have been a wonderful person."

"She was and this letter makes me miss her all the more." His voice broke at those words, and he wiped his eyes with his sleeve.

Rose didn't know what to do. She had never seen an almost grown up boy cry before. She wanted to hug him, like her mother would do to her, but felt it would not be proper. So she patted his arm trying to soothe him.

He quickly regained his composure. "I'm sorry for acting like a fool," he said. "I guess the letter affected me more than I thought it would."

"You have a right to be sad. After all, it *was* from your mother."

"You're so understanding, Rose. You won't tell…"

"And I won't tell anyone what happened," she interrupted.

"Thank you. And thank you too for reading the letter to me. You're a lot like her you know."

"Who?"

"My mother. You're kind and generous and understanding. And I'm sorry you will be getting off at Utica tonight. I'm going to miss you."

"I'm going to miss you too, Charles."

"But, I'll be coming back on this boat in three weeks when I go home to Albany."

"Good. Then I'll get to see you again and get to talk to you again." He seemed reluctant to let her go.

"You will."

"Great."

"I need to go back on the boat now, or Aunt Cora will think that I've disappeared."

"All right. Bye. And I hope you have a great time in Utica."

81

"Bye." Rose turned and walked back on the path, waving to Charles as she boarded the *Flying Eagle*.

"And what were you doin' out there?" Bridget's sharp voice startled her. She stood there with her hands on her hips looking Rose straight in the eye.

"Oh, I went out to say goodbye to Charles." Rose avoided looking directly at her. She couldn't tell her about the letter. She promised Charles.

"Do tell." Bridget wanted to yell at her to leave Charles alone, but she just bit her tongue and remained silent. She and Rose had just started being friends, and she didn't want to spoil things between them now. Besides, Rose would be gone when they got to Utica, and then she would have Charles all to herself.

"I thought you were going to pack your things," Bridget finally said.

"That's right. I never did do that. I better get to that right now." Rose scurried over to the clothes line and picked her now dry clothes off of it. She found her nearly dry carpetbag and neatly folded them into it. She just had her journal and a few more things downstairs to put in, and she would be ready to leave.

Chapter 10
Utica at Last

This is the last time I will write in this journal before I leave the boat. Then I must pack it away with my things. I will take it up again when I am settled with Aunt Jenny and Uncle Andrew in Utica. I am a little uneasy about meeting them and going off to live with them for three weeks. I hope they are as nice as Aunt Cora and Uncle Dermot.

I was also wary about this trip on the boat, and it turned out good at the end. Aunt Cora and Uncle Dermot have been like a second mother and father to me. I am happy that Bridget and I are friends, now, and that I met Charles. He is such a fine boy.

I wonder how Mama and Papa are and if Caleb's leg is healing. I do so miss them and the rest of the family. I will not see them in a long while yet.

Rose

With that Rose shut the book and tucked it carefully into the middle of the clothes in her carpetbag. It would be safe from harm there if her bag got tossed about the deck when she left. She fastened the buckles and set it down near her bunk.

When she stepped out of the room, Rose nearly collided with Sean who was shyly waiting there with his hands behind his back. "This is for you," he said as he held out a flat polished rock.

"Sean, I can't take that. It's your lucky stone." She squatted down to his height so she could look him in the eyes.

"But I want you to have it. It's a go away present."

"Oh," Rose was speechless. Then she hugged him. "Thank you, it's the nicest present anyone has ever given me." A tear escaped her eyes. "I'll take good care of it," she said as she slipped it into her dress pocket. She was going to miss Sean; he reminded her so much of Caleb.

As soon as Sean left, Rose spotted Tom coming down the stairs. "Well, cousin, I enjoyed meeting you and having you on the boat with us. I wanted to say goodbye in case I don't see you before you leave. It's my turn to take a sleep break now."

"Oh, Tom, it has been a wonderful trip, very different than I expected, but I did have fun."

"That's good. Bye, now." With that he entered the men's quarters to rest, so he could be ready for his next turn on the towpath.

Rose was beginning to feel very sad about leaving the Finnegans. She would miss them very much. She didn't think she could have become so fond of them in such a short time, but she did.

"Rose."

Rose turned at the sound of her name.

Aunt Cora stood there trying to be cheerful. "I know you'll be with Aunt Jenny and Uncle Andrew soon, and I know you'll have a wonderful time with them. I just want to tell you how much we enjoyed having you with us. I have a little something for you." She handed Rose a book and a box.

"Oh, Aunt Cora, a Godey's Lady's Book." Rose's eyes widened with delight when she saw the magazine. "I've always wanted one of those."

"It has all the latest fashions and styles in it."

Rose then lifted off the cover of the box. "Combs!" she cried out. As she held them up, she could see the tiny jewels sprinkled across the top, sparkling in the sunlight. "They're beautiful." Rose threw her arms around Aunt Cora and hugged her. "Thank you so much."

"It's the least I could do. You've been such a big help to us."

"You bought her combs!" Bridget shouted angrily. She had been coming down the stairs and witnessed everything. "How come you never bought *me* combs?" She sulked.

Bridget's outburst startled Rose since she had been so friendly lately.

"Bridget, I didn't think you'd want combs. You always wear your hair in braids," said Aunt Cora.

"That doesn't mean I don't want them," Bridget protested.

"Would you like one of these?" Rose tried to be helpful.

"*No*! I want my own!"

"Oh, all right, Bridget," said Aunt Cora, "Here!" She held out a box that was identical to the one she gave Rose. "I was going to save this for a Christmas present for you, but you better have it now."

Bridget's eyes widened. "You bought me combs? Oh, Mam, you're the best Mam in the entire world," she screamed and hugged her so tightly, she almost knocked her down. "I have to go try these on," she yelled as she disappeared into the sleeping quarters.

"Aunt Cora, I'm a little scared about going to Aunt Jenny's. My stomach gets queasy just thinking about it. I know it's silly, but I just can't help it."

"You'll be fine. You're just a little shy. I was like that when I was a girl, too. You were worried about this boat trip and it turned out fine, didn't it?"

"Oh, yes. I'm so happy to have met all of you."

"Your stay with Aunt Jenny will be fine, too."

"Thank you. I always feel better when I talk to you, Aunt Cora."

"Well, I have to go and see how near we are to Utica. I'll be on deck if you need me."

"All right."

Rose decided to look in on Bridget to see how she was doing, arranging her hair with the combs. She pulled aside the curtain to the room and looked in. She had all she could do to keep from laughing when she saw Bridget sitting on the bunk with her hair sticking straight up and out, all over her head.

"Do you need some help?" Rose laughed not being able to hold it back any more.

"Stop laughin' at me, Rose Stewart!" Bridget shouted. "I just can't do this!"

"Do you need some help? Let's look in the Godey's Lady's Book for some hair styles." Rose laid the book on the bunk.

"That's a good idea," said Bridget, sounding a little less frustrated.

They leafed through the pages until Bridget found something she liked.

"Can you make it look like that?"

"I'll try." Rose swept Bridget's hair up and twisted it into a small topknot on the back of her head. She positioned the combs in place to hold it up and pulled a few strands of hair out in front of her ears.

"There," Rose said when she was finished, standing back to admire her creation.

Bridget ran over to the mirror to look. "Is that me? It's beautiful. I'm beautiful!" She looked at least fifteen years old. Wait till Charles saw her now. "Thank you, Rose," she shouted as she hugged her cousin. "I'm going to miss you so much. I really wish you didn't have to go to Utica right now."

"I'll miss you too, but we'll see each other on the trip back. I'm glad we're friends at last."

"Me, too."

Aunt Cora came running down the stairs. "We've arrived. We're in Utica, girls. Uncle Dermot docked the boat and is looking for Uncle Andrew."

When they reached the deck, they saw Uncle Dermot talking to a tall, handsome, dark-haired man. "Come here, girls, I want you to meet someone," he boomed when he saw them.

Rose felt her stomach tighten but kept following Bridget to where the men were standing.

"This is your Uncle Andrew, Rose. His horse and wagon and tied up on the street."

"Hello," Rose said feeling uneasy.

"Hello, Rose. We are looking forward to your visit." Uncle Andrew smiled at her. "Aunt Jenny can't wait to meet you."

"Charles can put your things in the wagon, Rose," said Uncle Dermot. "We're not going to stop to visit now since Jenny is still under the weather from the birth, and I need to get this cargo to Syracuse. We'll stop in when we pick Rose up, and Jenny is feeling better."

"Sure. That's probably a good idea. I've got that desk you said you'd deliver to my brother in Syracuse," said

Uncle Andrew, "but I'll need some help getting it down to the boat from my wagon."

"Charles can help with that too," said Uncle Dermot.

Charles appeared as soon as he was called and went off with Uncle Andrew to get the desk. Before long, they were loading it onto the boat.

"I can't thank you enough for doing me this favor. My brother will be forever grateful," said Uncle Andrew when the task was done, "and now it's time to go."

They all said their goodbyes and hugged again, and then Rose left with Uncle Andrew.

"Rose, wait a minute." It was Charles.

She turned and walked back to where he was standing. "What do you want?" she asked.

"Oh..." he looked sheepish. "I just wanted to say one more goodbye." With that, his lips brushed her forehead, and he ran back to the boat, waving at her, shouting, "See you in three weeks."

Uncle Andrew was several yards ahead of her and waited when Charles called her back. "Is that your young man?" he asked when she caught up to him.

Rose blushed at the words. She was glad it was dark, so Uncle Andrew couldn't see her face. "He's just a friend," she said.

"Well, here's my wagon. I'll help you up."

Rose was quiet on the way home. All she could do was fret about this new place. Would she ever be able to look at things the way Bridget did? Why did she have to worry so?

"We're here," Uncle Andrew's voice interrupted her thoughts. "I'll bring your things in later. I'm sure you'll want to meet Aunt Jenny and the boys first." He helped her down from the wagon.

Bridget's words echoed in her mind. *The more you do the things you're scared of, the less scared you'll be.* She vowed to remember that.

Uncle Andrew opened the front door of the house. "We're here, Jenny, come and meet Rose," he said.

With that a slim woman came to the door.

When she saw her, Rose's eyes widened and her mouth dropped open. She wanted to yell, "Mama," but she just stared.

Aunt Jenny looked so much like her mother she could have been her twin. She had the same red hair, the same green eyes, the same fair complexion, and the same way about her that her mother had. Rose knew now that things would be just fine in Utica. They would be excellent.

American Life in 1840

In 1840, Martin Van Buren was president of the United States, and Richard Johnson was vice president. That was the year the postage stamp was developed. A popular novel of that time was, *Two Years Before the Mast* by Richard Henry Dana. *America* and *Amazing Grace* were popular songs.

Life was very different then from what it is now. People had to do without many of the modern conveniences we have today. There was no TV, no radio, no telephone, no microwave, no stereo, no central heating, and no air conditioning.

Candles and gas lamps lighted homes since there was no electricity yet. Fireplaces and wood stoves, which usually went out in the middle of the night, provided heat. Water had to be hauled from pumps or wells.

The woman of the house performed all of the chores. She did washing by hand, sewing of all the families clothing, preserving food, cooking, cleaning, and caring for five to seven children. Baths were taken in tin tubs on the kitchen floor with water heated on the stove.

A typical breakfast consisted of buckwheat pancakes with maple syrup; oatmeal; or eggs, sausages, and toast along with light tea or coffee. Lunch, called dinner, might be beef, buttered potatoes, turnips, pie, and strong tea. Supper would be similar to dinner. Drying, smoking, salting, and pickling, were methods used to preserve food.

The women of the family sewed most of the clothing. Ladies wore long bell shaped dresses with bustles, and frequently used shawls. They also liked to wear turbans. Girls usually wore aprons over their dresses to keep them clean. Levis jeans came out in the mid 1800's.

People earned their living in many different ways. Most of them worked on farms. Others were blacksmiths, chimney sweeps, coopers, lamplighters, peddlers, barbers, barkeepers, cobblers, and sextons. The hours were long and the pay was poor. When women and children worked, they were paid much less than men were.

Barter and trade were often used instead of money before 1840. After that, America gradually went to a money system.

Hot air balloons, bicycle riding, and bowling were all popular amusements of the '40s. People liked to play cards, billiards, and checkers. They enjoyed music, the theater, dancing, and visiting each other. In the winter, sleigh riding was a favorite pastime.

Transportation was difficult and slow due to poor roads that often turned muddy in the spring. Land travel was by horse, wagon, stagecoach, and after 1835, railroads. Stagecoaches usually tipped over at least once on a long trip, making it a tormenting experience. Water travel was by boat on a river or canal.

Doctors were trained by the apprentice system and most did not have degrees. Many people depended on herbs and folk medicine since doctors were not always handy. There were no antibiotics, or anesthesia for surgery. Children had a high death rate due to problems with childbirth and from childhood diseases.

Reference:
McCutcheon, Marc, *Everyday Life in the 1800's*, Writer's Digest Books, 1993.

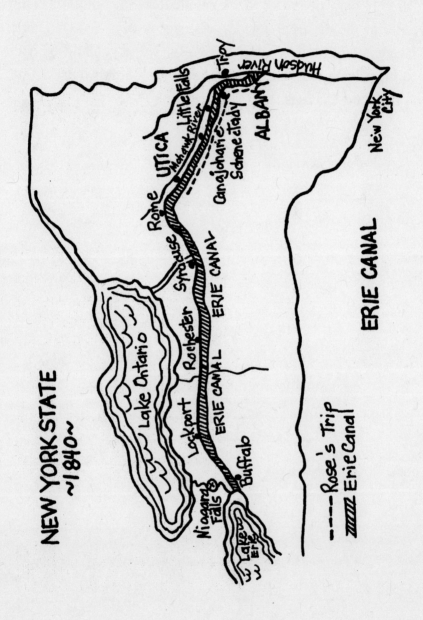

NEW YORK STATE
~1840~

Lake Ontario

Lake Erie

Niagara Falls

Buffalo

Lockport

ERIE CANAL

Rochester

Syracuse

ERIE CANAL

Rome   UTICA

Mohawk River

Little Falls

Canajoharie

Schenectady

Troy

ALBANY

Hudson River

New York City

ERIE CANAL

- - - Rose's Trip
///// Erie Canal

94

Erie Canal Facts and Timeline

The Erie Canal is a 363-mile man-made waterway across New York State between Buffalo and Albany. It was 40 feet wide and four feet deep when first built. It consisted of 83 locks and had 300 bridges between Albany and Utica. The canal took eight years to build at a cost of over seven million dollars.

Travel on the Erie Canal made it possible to go from Albany to Buffalo in ten days whereas using the land route would have taken two to three weeks.

The canal was eventually enlarged to 70 feet wide and seven feet deep.

❖ **early 1800** – Interest in a canal for easier transportation across the state, begins.

❖ **1808** – New York State Legislature decides to have a survey of possible canal routes.

❖ **1817** - Canal is approved of by New York State Legislature in April.

❖ **1817** - Digging begins on the Erie Canal at Rome, New York on July 4[th.]

❖ **1819** –Stretch of the Canal between Utica and Rome is completed and opened.

❖ **1825** – Canal is finished.
Ceremonies including *Wedding of the Waters* take place in October.

❖ **1836 to 1862** - Enlargement of the canal takes place.

1840's Lingo

canawlers – men who lived and worked on the canals

candle-lighting time – just before darkness, dusk

carpetbag – a traveling bag made of left-over carpet
         pieces

cholera – a disease causing diarrhea and dehydration,
         often resulting in death within hours

Clinton's Ditch, Clinton's Folly – names for Erie Canal
    associating it with De Witt Clinton, a big supporter of it

consumption – tuberculosis, a lung destroying illness

crocks – thick stoneware pots or jars

Da – Irish name for Father

do tell – tell me more

Godey's Lady's Book – a popular lady's fashion
         magazine first called, *Lady's Book*

Grand Canal – early name for the Erie Canal

hankering – desiring, wanting

Mam – Irish name for Mother

man alive – surprise

McGuffey reader – grade-leveled, eclectic readers for children, first published in 1836

Montezuma Swamp – swampy area past Syracuse said to harbor ghosts

pile on the agony – adding insult to injury

rambunctious – very active

reckon – to think

rip-roaring – exciting, thrilling

sakes alive – for heaven's sake

tuckered out –extremely tired, exhausted

uppity – snobbish, snooty

wishing on a hayload – like wishing on a star

Yorkers – residents of New York State

Reference:
McCutcheon, Marc, *Everyday Life in the 1800's*, Writer's Digest Books, 1993.